MATT CHRISTOPHER

Baseball Jokes and Riddles

Illustrated by Daniel Vasconcellos

Little, Brown and Company
Boston   New York   Toronto   London

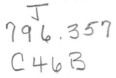
First Edition

Library of Congress Cataloging-in-Publication Data

Christopher, Matt.
    Baseball jokes and riddles / Matt Christopher ; illustrated by Daniel
Vasconcellos. — 1st ed.
        p.   cm.
    Summary: A collection of jokes, riddles, and humorous anecdotes about the game of baseball.
    ISBN 0-316-14081-3
    1. Baseball — Juvenile humor. [1. Baseball — Wit and humor. 2. Riddles. 3. Jokes.]
I. Vasconcellos, Daniel, ill. II. Title.
PN6231.B35C37   1996
796.357'0207 — dc20   95-19883

10   9   8   7   6   5   4   3   2   1

B P

Published simultaneously in Canada by Little, Brown & Company (Canada) Limited

Printed in the United States of America

To Michelle Elizabeth—M. C.

To my wife, Joan, and
my daughter, Nora—D. V.

Catcher: You're missing the strike zone by a mile! Better get your eyes checked.

Pitcher: Whenever I pitch against the Twins, I see double!

Catcher: You look a little nervous out there today.

Pitcher: Whenever I pitch against the Cubs, I just can't *bear* it!

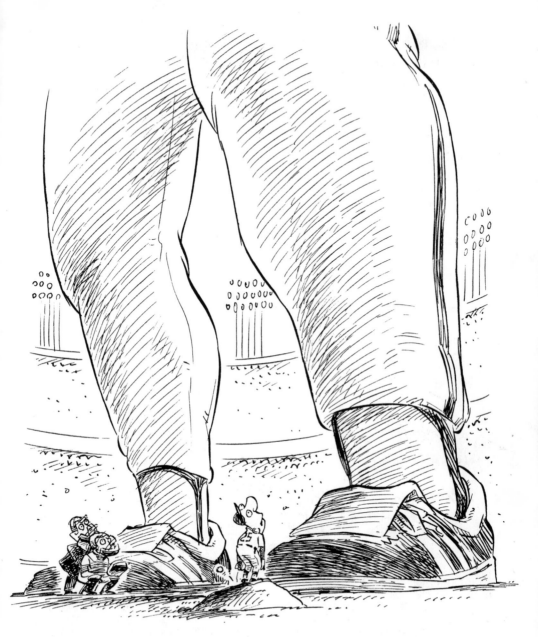

Catcher: You seem to be lacking confidence today.

Pitcher: Whenever I pitch against the Giants, I always feel kind of small!

What is the best country for an official scorekeeper to live in?

The United *Stats!*

In what state do most umpires live?

In New York, the Umpire State!

First Baseman: Why did the pitcher throw a baseball across the table?

Second Baseman: The manager told him to put one over the plate!

In what ballpark are players most nimble and quick?

Candlestick Park!

What is the best day of the week to play a doubleheader?

Twos-day!

What does an umpire do before he eats?

Brushes off the plate!

Why are babies good at fielding ground balls?
They're good at little dribblers!

Why is a sold-out ballpark a good place to go on a hot day?

Because there's a fan in every seat!

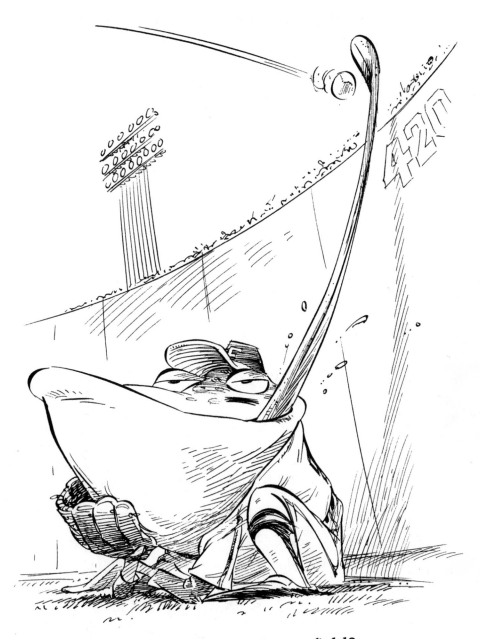

Why is it good to have frogs in the outfield?
They never miss a fly!

Mistaken Identity

California Angels infielder Aurelio Rodriguez was in for a surprise when he saw his 1969 Topps baseball card. When the photographer from Topps visited spring training camp, he mistook the Angels batboy for Rodriguez — and took *his* picture instead! So all of Rodriguez's Topps cards that season featured a picture of the batboy!

(Very) Short Sleeves

Reds first baseman Ted Kluszewski (played 1946–1961) had such muscular arms, he had to cut the sleeves of his uniform to get into it!

Charley Horse

Pitcher Charley Esper, who played with Baltimore in the 1890s, was not known for his breakaway running speed. In fact, his teammates thought he ran like a lame horse. Ever since, a runner who suffers from a cramp in his leg is said to have a "charley horse"!

And Stepping Up to the Chatter's Box . . .

St. Louis Brown Arlie Latham was unofficially known as the father of "chatter" — baseball's time-honored tradition of nonstop talk. Called "The Freshest Man on Earth," Latham was once offered a box of silk socks and underwear if he could remain quiet for a whole game. He couldn't.

Mr. Excitement

Long-ball hitter Harmon Killebrew (573 lifetime homers) of the old Washington Senators was a solid ballplayer — but he wasn't a very exciting guy off the field. When asked what his hobbies were, he replied, "Well, I like to wash the dishes, I guess." He was also known for his good handwriting.

Is That Mummy Pitching Today?

Yankee pitcher Jim Coates, who played in the 1950s, slept with his eyes open, earning him the nickname "Mummy"!

All Horror Team

Mitch "The Wild Thing" Williams

Phil "The Vulture" Regan

Jim "Mummy" Coates

Dick "The Monster" Radatz

The "Green Monster" of Boston's Fenway Park

Right Fielder: I can never find any bats during a day game.

Left Fielder: Why is that?

Right Fielder: Because bats come out only at night!

First Baseman: What's the count?

Second Baseman: Some guy from Transylvania!

First Baseman: What did the pitcher do when the count was one and two?

Second Baseman: Nothing. He didn't know him then.

First Baseman: What did the pitcher do when the count was full?

Second Baseman: Burp him!

Hat Trick

When Orioles pitcher Mike Cuellar and the team arrived in Milwaukee for a series, he informed manager Earl Weaver that he had forgotten his lucky baseball cap. Even though Cuellar was on a nine-game winning streak, he felt he would lose the next night without it. In those days there was no overnight delivery — but with the help of the Orioles front office, the airlines, and a series of hand deliveries, the hat was delivered to Cuellar before game time. Cuellar's first words upon opening the box? "They sent my *practice* cap!" (Cuellar lasted only three innings that night!)

Going a Bit Batty

Ballplayers are a superstitious lot, especially when it comes to their bats and hitting. Orlando Cepeda believed that each bat had only one hit — so after every hit, he got a new bat! And Wade Boggs gets rid of a bat when he feels he has used up its supply of hits!

The Eyes Have It

Many ballplayers have their rituals that they believe bring them good luck. Fay Dancer, center fielder for the Peoria, Illinois, Redwings of the All-American Girls Professional Baseball League, would pry the glass eyes out of merry-go-round horses and give them to fans to rub for good luck!

Look Out!

When Hall of Fame pitcher Grover Cleveland Alexander was accused of throwing an illegal beanball at a batter, he replied, "All I did was throw a curve, but it kept following him!"

Ground Ball

At old Griffith Stadium in Washington, D.C., in a game
between the Senators and the Tigers, Detroit's George
Kell was up at the plate. The pitcher was in his windup
when the lights suddenly went out! When they blinked
back on a few seconds later, everyone on the field was
lying down, protecting their heads! Only the pitcher and
Kell knew for sure if the ball had been thrown — no one
wanted to get hit by a pitch or a line drive!

Fashion Firsts

Stolen base specialist Lou Brock knew what to wear during a rain delay. He had an interest in a company that made the BroccaBrella, a small umbrella worn like a hat!

In 1976, the White Sox tried out knee-length shorts, but quickly decided to go back to long pants — maybe their runners weren't sliding into bases! (Ouch!)

Risky Business

Before 1877, players risked serious injury when sliding into a base. It wasn't until that year that the standard fifteen-inch canvas covered bag was adopted — before then, some ball fields used flat stones or wooden stakes!

Being Taken *to the* Cleaners

When the Boston Braves won their 1946 season opener against the Brooklyn Dodgers, not all of their 18,261 fans went home happy. It seems the Braves had decided to spruce up Fenway before the game by giving the stands a fresh coat of paint. Cold, wet weather prevented the paint from drying in some grandstand sections — so three hundred unlucky patrons took home more than happy memories from the game! (The next day the team ran ads in the newspapers offering to pay the dry cleaning bills!)

All Zoo Team

Mule Haas

Bill "Moose" Skowron

Johnny "The Big Cat" Mize

Jimmie Foxx

Harvey "The Kitten" Haddix

Jim "Catfish" Hunter

Rob Deer

Lou "The Iron Horse" Gehrig

What did the chicken say to the pitcher?
Baalk, balk, balk, balk, baalk!

Why were the players wearing armor at the ballpark?

It was a knight game!

What are the best kind of shoes to wear for stealing bases?
Sneakers!

What is the best kind of pitch to steal on?
A slider!

Spelling B (Or B-)

In 1967, future Hall of Famer Carl Yastrzemski was voted the best player in baseball by his fellow major leaguers. The ballots, however, showed that while many of the voters may have excelled in baseball, their spelling left much to be desired! Written in were such entries as:

Yaztremski   Yaztreszski

Yastremzminski   Yastremski

Yazstrememenski   Y'str'mski

(The smart ones played it safe and wrote: *Yaz — Boston!*)

What's the Dirt?

Phillies first baseman Richie Allen wrote messages in the dirt as his way of protesting bad calls. Baseball Commissioner Bowie Kuhn told the Phillies to make Allen stop. When he heard of Kuhn's order, Allen wrote three more messages: *No, Why,* and *Mom.* When asked why he wrote *Mom,* he replied, "To say she tells me what to do, not the man up there."

"Home Run" or "Run Home"?

When New York Met Jimmy Piersall, a player known for his on-the-field antics, ran around the bases after hitting his one hundredth career home run on June 23, 1963, he ran them in order — but backwards!

The Shortest Distance

Oakland A's pinch runner Allan Lewis, known as "The Panamanian Express," once tried to score from second base — by way of the pitcher's mound!

Bert-Ball

On September 8, 1965, Bert Campaneris made major league history by becoming the first player to play all nine positions — in one game!

Fowl Play!

St. Louis Browns pitcher Ellis Kinder was happy he was playing "heads up" ball in a game against the Red Sox in 1947. If he hadn't been, he would have been hit by a fish that a seagull dropped on the mound! (Could it be the seagull was a Red Sox fan?)

Heads Up!

In a game at Cleveland Stadium on May 26, 1993, Jose Canseco, then a Texas Ranger, went up against the outfield fence to snag a long ball hit by Carlos Martinez. Jose missed the ball with his glove — but the ball didn't miss him. It bounced off his head and popped over the fence for a home run!

All Fowl Team

Joe "Ducky" Medwick

Goose Gossage

Mark "The Bird" Fidrych

Robin Roberts

Goose Goslin

Rick
"Rooster"
Burleson

Manager: Why are you holding your ribs?
Base Runner: I was caught in a squeeze play!

Trainer: You look a little dragged out.

Base Runner: I was just run down between second and third.

All Crayon Team

Red Rolfe

Bill White

Mordecai Brown

Vida Blue

Mail Call

By the end of the 1973 season, Hank Aaron was just one home run short of tying Babe Ruth's 714 home run record. But he *had* broken another record already: He had received 930,000 pieces of mail, more mail than any other American except the president of the United States!

Sign Language

Future Hall of Fame pitcher Bob Gibson of the Cardinals broke his leg during the pennant race of 1967. He grew tired of answering the same questions over and over, so he taped a sheet of paper to his shirtfront with this message:

1. Yes, it's off.
2. No, it doesn't hurt.
3. I don't know how much longer.

Double Play

In 1934, Moe Berg was invited to Japan as a third-string catcher of the American League All-Star team. While the game was going on, Moe did a strange thing. He dressed in a black kimono and climbed to the roof of a nearby hospital to take pictures of Tokyo. Moe was simply taking time out for his other, part-time job — as a spy for the United States government!

A Close Call

When Al Lopez managed the Chicago White Sox, he had the club purchase a World War II submarine periscope from war surplus. It was installed in the Comiskey Park scoreboard in dead center field so a "spy" could steal the catcher's signs of the visiting team. The "spy" phoned the information to Lopez in the dugout!

All Cooking Team

Spud Chandler

Bob Lemon

Ty "The Georgia Peach" Cobb

Jim Rice

Darryl
Strawberry

Cookie
Lavagetto

Zach Wheat

Candy
Maldonado

Pepper
Martin

Unfundamentals of Baseball

Keep your eye on the ball!

Cover second!

A first baseman holds a runner at first.

Caught stealing!

Nice catch!